ROSE

the cat-dog

ISBN: 978-1-7368490-0-2

**Don't forget to follow Rose and her family's adventures
on Instagram @rosethecatdog**

Connect by DM or at rosethecatdog@gmail.com

ROSE
the cat-dog

Written by
Todd Albert

Illustrated by
Sirma Karaguiozova

To Rose, who taught us that there is strength in our so-called weakness.

To Maeve & Freya, for being the best little human sisters a cat-dog could ask for.

Rose is a cat-dog.

Now, I'm not saying that Rose actually *IS* a cat, but she sure acts a lot like one.

☑ She keeps to herself.

☑ She *LOVES* to lick her paws.

 She does **NOT** play fetch.

 Her favorite way **TO** play is by rolling around on top of other people's stuff (although she does tire out pretty quickly).

3

She only eats until full (never more).

and . . .

She most certainly does not like going for walks.

Don't get me wrong. I know not all cats are like this. Even so, Rose's family usually thought of her as more like your average cat than dog because of all of her unique behavior.

So, as much as Rose may not have liked it - and she really did not like it - her family took her for walks anyway. One day, on just such a walk to the park, Rose overheard two dogs talking:

My humans have a baby on the way.

As dogs, it's our duty to **PROTECT** them, **PLAY** with them...

Mine too!

and **LOVE** them too!!!

6

Rose was listening very closely from nearby.

"Oh no," she thought to herself, "my humans also have a baby on the way and I don't know how to do any of those dog-like things!"

Rose thought this way because she'd had a very different type of puppyhood than most of the other dogs she knew.

You see, Rose was a rescue dog. Rescue dogs come from different types of places - sometimes from homes that just can't keep them anymore, but often from places that are really not that good at all. That is why they need to be "rescued" or saved by people like Rose's humans or by special organizations dedicated to finding them new homes.

In Rose's case, she was rescued from a **REALLY** not-so-nice place. She never had any toys, treats, hugs, room to play, or even a name! Because of this, she also never learned everyday dog things. Instead, acting like a cat-dog had kept her safe, and that is why she developed such careful and quiet feline ways. It was a hard habit to break, even after she joined her humans in their **FUR**ever home.

8

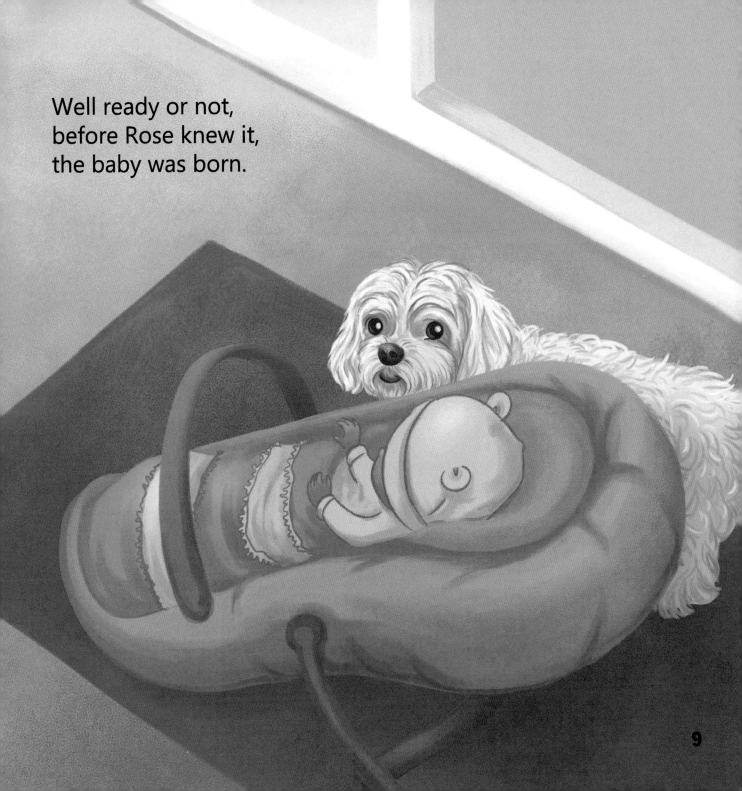

Well ready or not,
before Rose knew it,
the baby was born.

9

Now, Rose knew that her humans were ok with her just the way she was since they were the ones who had rescued her.

But now she was the baby's dog too. Taking one look at her new little human sister, Rose decided right then and there that she couldn't be her cat-dog self any longer. Instead, she would have to start acting like those dogs in the park. The only problem was that Rose didn't know **HOW** to be like other dogs, but she was determined to figure it out!

Rose's first chance to try came unexpectedly that very afternoon.

Everything was quiet. The baby had just gone done for a nap, and then someone knocked gently on the apartment door.

Upon hearing this, Rose thought "I guess this is my chance to **PROTECT** my little human sister from the sound that's going to wake her up!" So Rose ran down the hallway - **BARKING** all the way - to let whoever it was know to stop making so much noise.

But it was Rose's barking that woke the baby.

Rose decided she would have to keep trying to act more like a "regular" dog and not her usual cat-dog self until she got it right.

13

Time passed. The baby grew and learned to sit up. And Rose kept trying. But like I said, old habits are hard to break and cat-dogs **REALLY** like their alone time.

Rose knew that dogs are supposed to **PLAY** with their little human sisters too. Still, she just didn't think things like chasing balls were that much fun (remember? She does **NOT** play fetch).

Rose never did manage to bring back the ball, which made the baby cry.

15

All of the crying was making Rose upset and annoyed with herself. Even though she really did **LOVE** the baby, she never seemed to have enough energy to play with her the way she thought she should.

She tried to make things better by sharing one of her own favorite activities with the baby. Even so, it seems like babies don't love having their "paws" licked all the time. It would make the baby cry every time Rose tried (and tried and tried).

Sticky baby hands and feet sure are tasty,
Rose thought as she tried yet again.

One day, Rose was in a particularly good mood. She didn't know if it was because ...

...she'd had a great night's sleep after squeezing herself under her humans' bed to get away from them when they tried to trim her nails,

...or that she had been lucky enough to come across some freshly cleaned and still warm towels to roll around on top of after an especially cold, wet and unpleasant walk.

Whatever the reason, Rose decided to share her happiness with the baby by giving her some "Rose kisses."

Rose kisses were Rose's way of showing love. She would give them by going up to someone and rubbing and bumping her head against whichever part of the person she could reach over and over again. So far only her two humans had been lucky enough to receive them.

17

Rose found the baby sitting on the couch, eating snacks out of a bowl in her lap. Rose was in such a good mood, she ran right up her doggy steps and over to the baby, giving her some really strong and wholehearted Rose kisses on the arm.

At first the baby laughed because Rose had never done anything like this before, and it kind of tickled anyway, but then all of the head bumping toppled the baby over onto her side! Her bowl fell to the floor, spilling treats everywhere.

The baby's laughter became loud cries of unhappiness.

Rose felt bad. That did not go as planned. Still, she hopped off the couch and ate up all the treats. A cat-dog knows to never let good food go to waste.

This only made the baby cry even more.

Nothing Rose did seemed to be working. Everything she tried just made the baby cry. She wondered why wanting to **PROTECT**, **PLAY** with and **LOVE** the baby was turning out to be so hard.

Unsure of what to do next, Rose headed to her favorite place under the living room end table to do some thinking.

Rose spent a lot of time under that table over many days and weeks trying to figure out what to do next.

(Well, she would have been under there a lot anyway since it was her favorite place to get away from everyone. Still, she did do a lot of extra thinking about the baby and how to be a good dog while down there.)

On Halloween, the family was getting ready to go trick-or-treating. Rose was under the table again, feeling sad about not behaving like the type of dog she thought she needed to be. She didn't want to go anywhere. All the same, her family took her along as usual.

As they walked from house to house, the baby sucked on her binky, which was her most favorite thing in the world. Then, the worst thing that could ever happen, happened. While leaning over the stroller and looking back at some passing kids in bright costumes, the baby sneezed and her binky shot out of her mouth and onto the ground behind her, bouncing out of sight from everyone, including her parents, who were looking the other way!

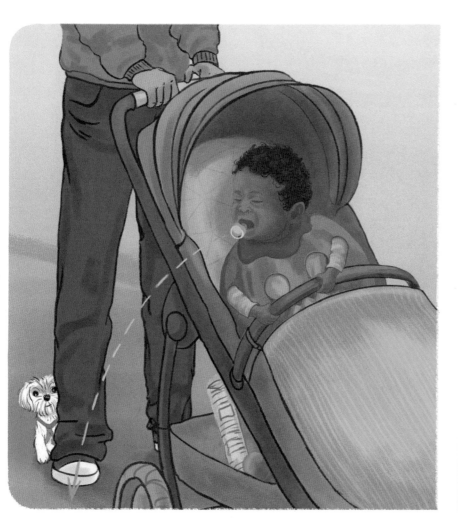

Out of sight to everyone, that is, except for Rose, who had been hiding behind her humans to avoid a group of young trick-or-treaters who wanted to pet her (you'd probably not be surprised to learn that Rose did not enjoy meeting new people).

The binky stopped its bouncing right under Rose's nose. The baby had already begun to fuss about it, nearly in tears. Looking from the binky to the baby and back again, Rose suddenly realized:

"I can **PROTECT** the baby if I get the binky back to her before she starts crying!"

With her heart swelling with **LOVE**, Rose did the only thing she could think of next - she began to **PLAY** with the binky by dropping down and rolling around on top of it with all of her might.

Rose's humans had forgotten the backup binky at home, and were now franticly searching the area in front of the stroller.

They stopped when they noticed Rose rolling around on top of something like she had never rolled around on top of something before.

Knowing Rose, they knew it had to be something really important for her to move like that. She didn't even seem to be tiring out yet, which must have been a new record for her! At home, that would mean it was probably something like a cell phone or a favorite, newly cleaned sweater underneath her.

Could it be the binky now since they were out here on the street?

Once they got Rose to stop - boy, she really did love a good roll on top of important stuff - it **WAS** the binky underneath her!

Seeing this, the baby's fussing stopped immediately, replaced by a toothless smile from ear to ear. What the baby did next was something she had never done before:

Instead of reaching for her binky, she reached for Rose!

Rose is a cat-dog.

By being herself,
she saved the day.

EPILOGUE

More time passed. The baby is older now.

She even has a little sister who is not so small herself anymore.

Even after all this time, though, Rose is still her cat-dog self. And the girls **LOVE** her for it. They **PROTECT** her and **PLAY** with her just the way she likes it - *not too much*.

Made in the USA
Las Vegas, NV
20 June 2021